I AM THE HULK

Adaptation by Acton Figueroa
Based on the motion picture screenplay
written by James Schamus
Illustrations by James Goodridge

HarperFestival®
A Division of HarperCollins*Publishers*

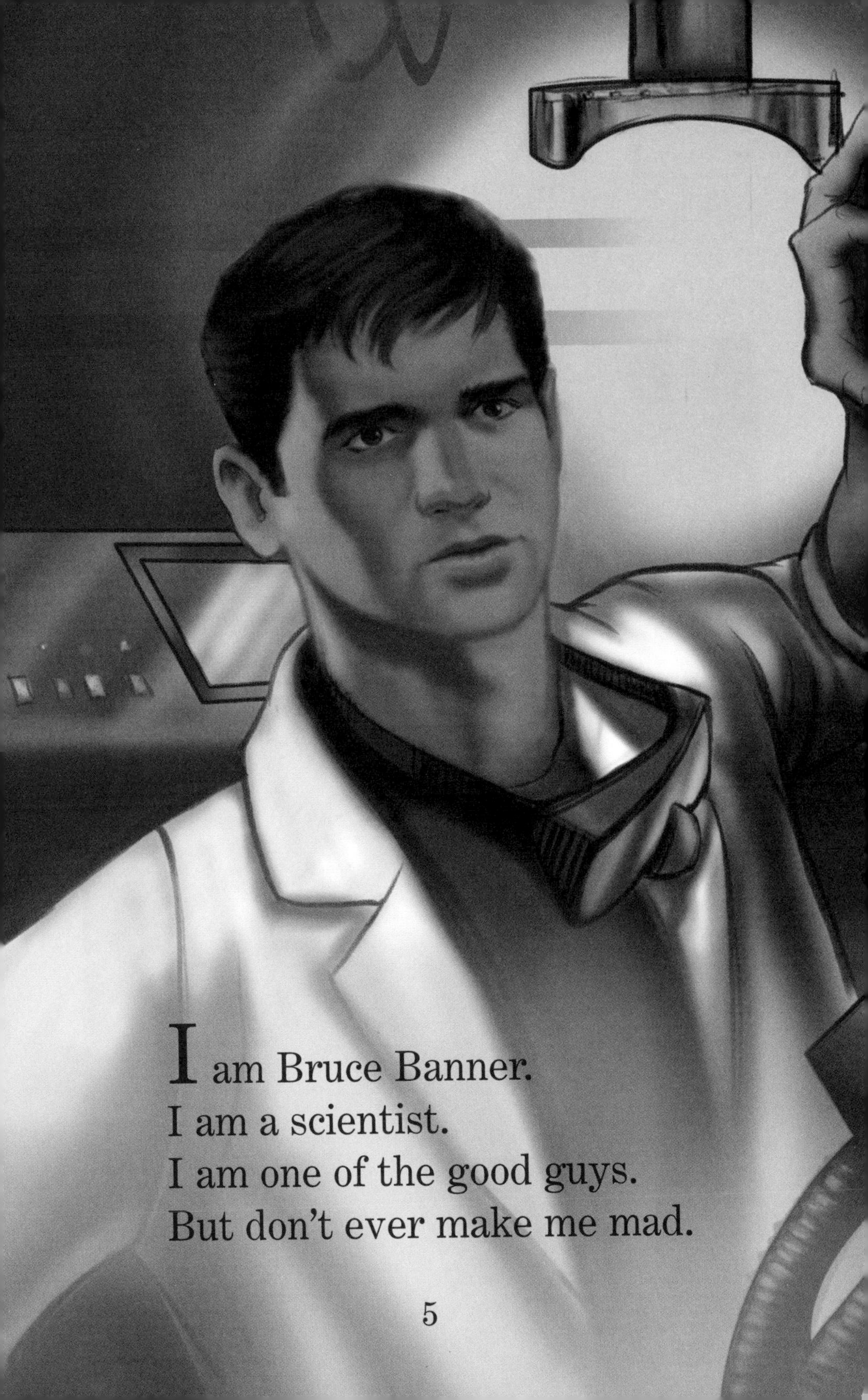

I am Bruce Banner.
I am a scientist.
I am one of the good guys.
But don't ever make me mad.

I'm different from you.
I don't look different.
Not yet.
But I am.

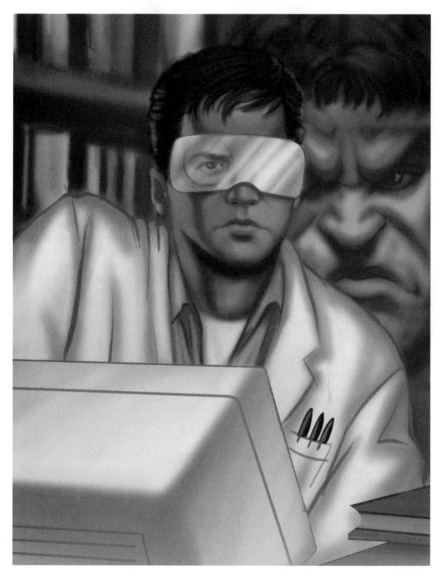

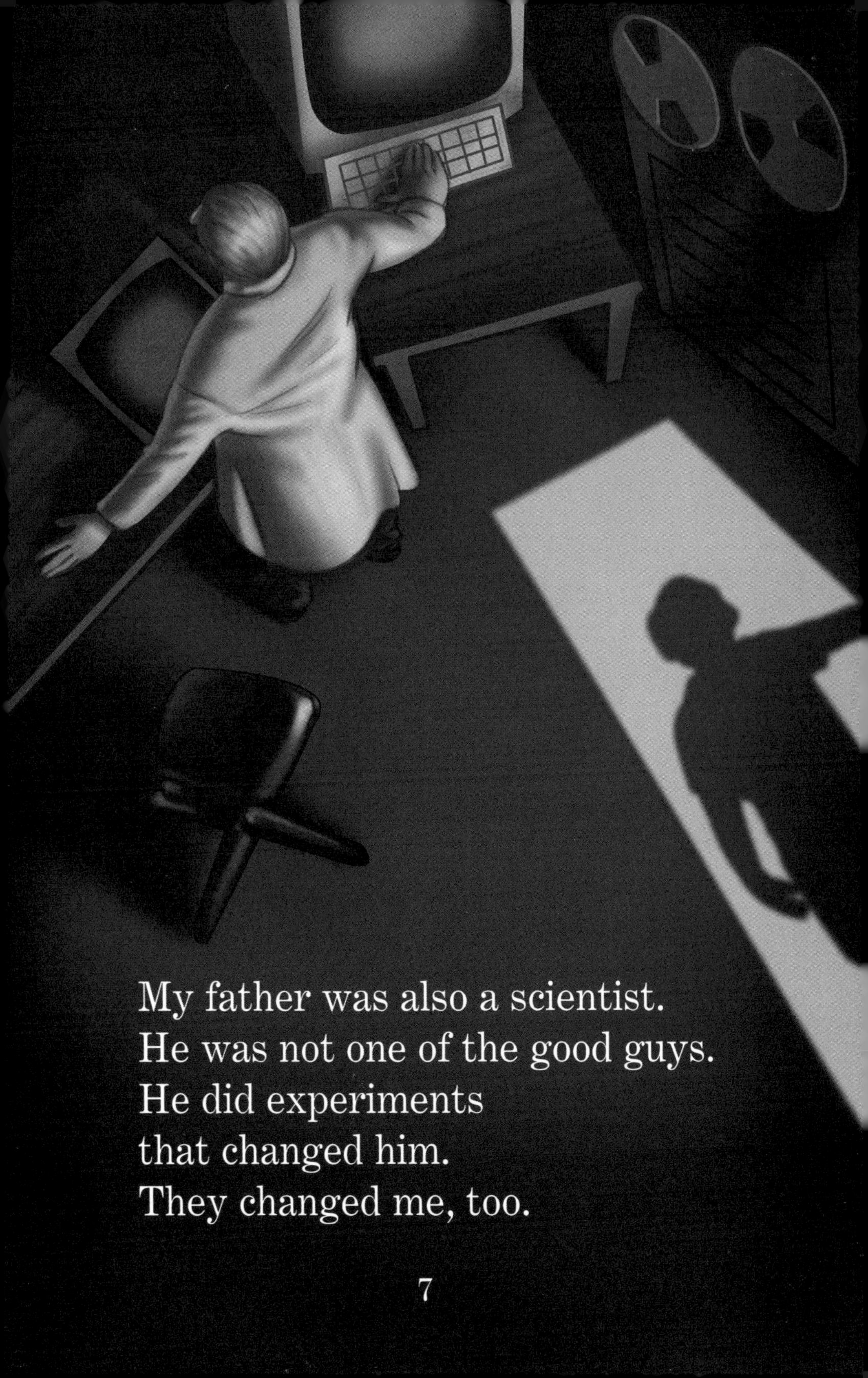

My father was also a scientist.
He was not one of the good guys.
He did experiments
that changed him.
They changed me, too.

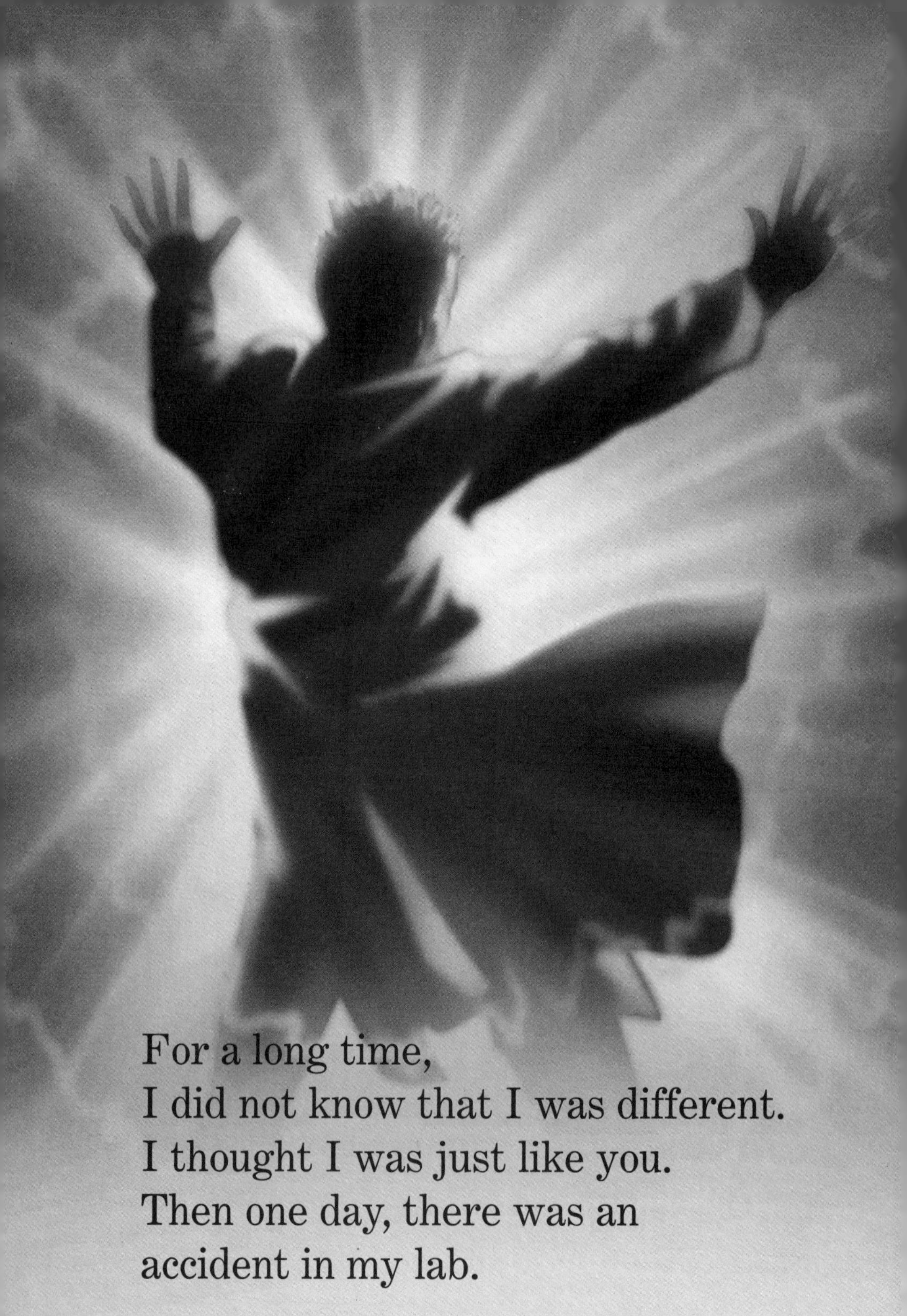

For a long time,
I did not know that I was different.
I thought I was just like you.
Then one day, there was an
accident in my lab.

I saved my friends,
but I couldn't save myself.
After the accident,
I was never the same.
Now, when I get mad,
I change . . . into the Hulk!

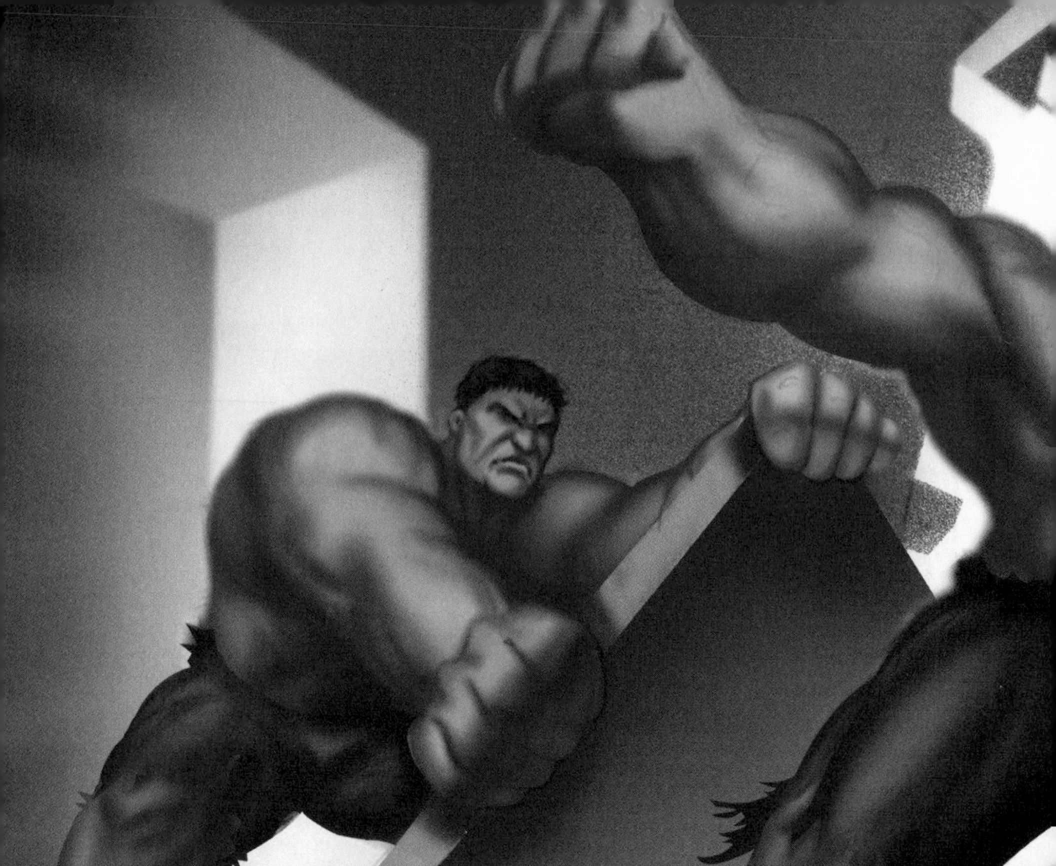

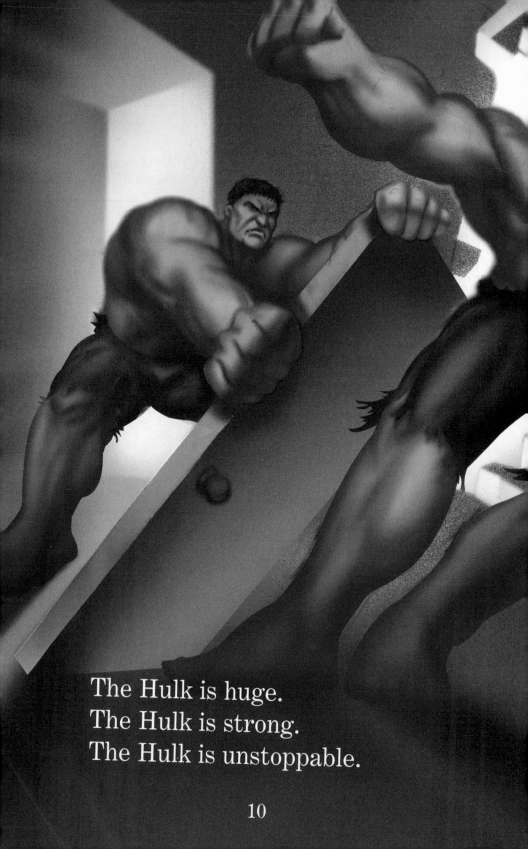

The Hulk is huge.
The Hulk is strong.
The Hulk is unstoppable.

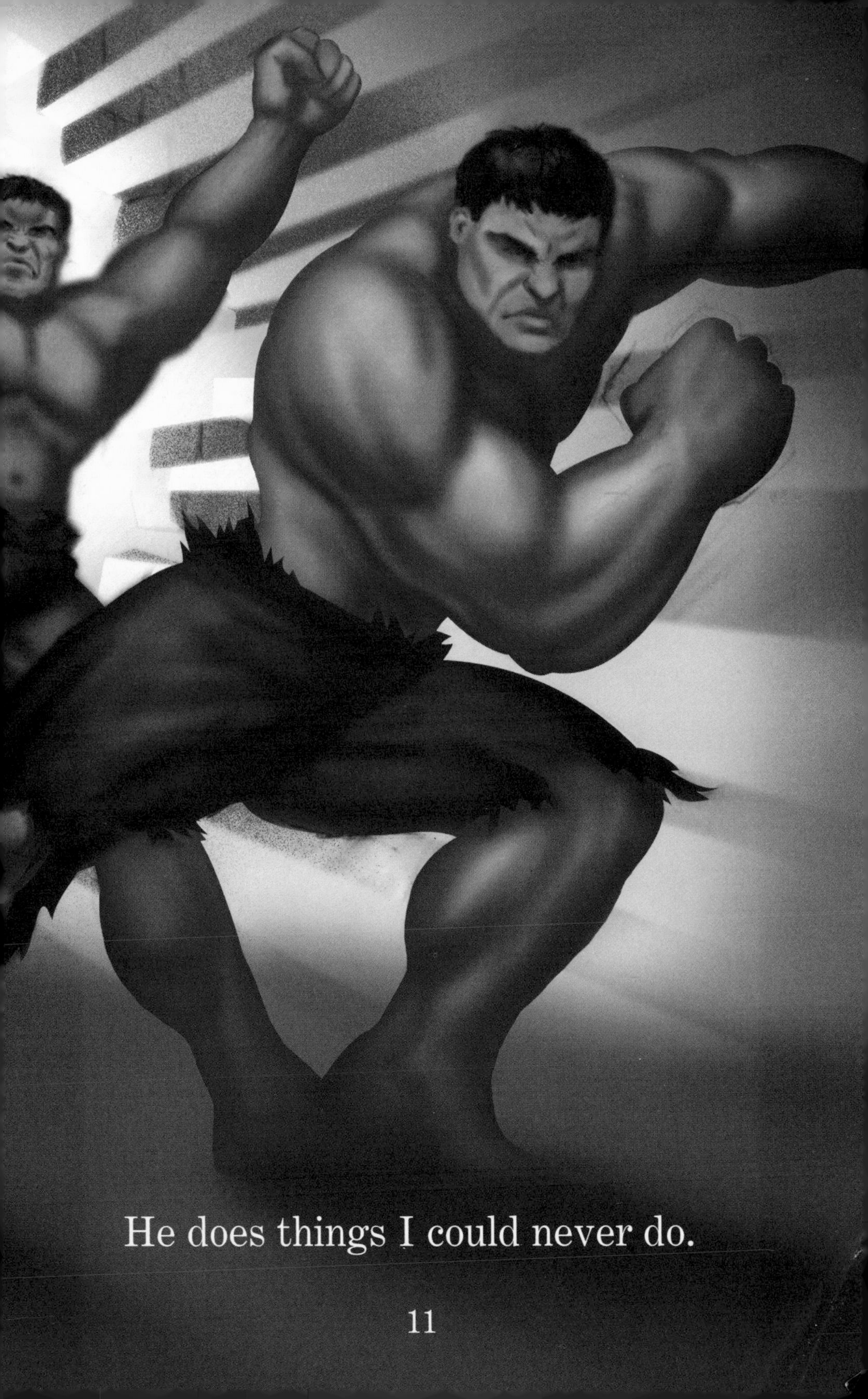

He does things I could never do.

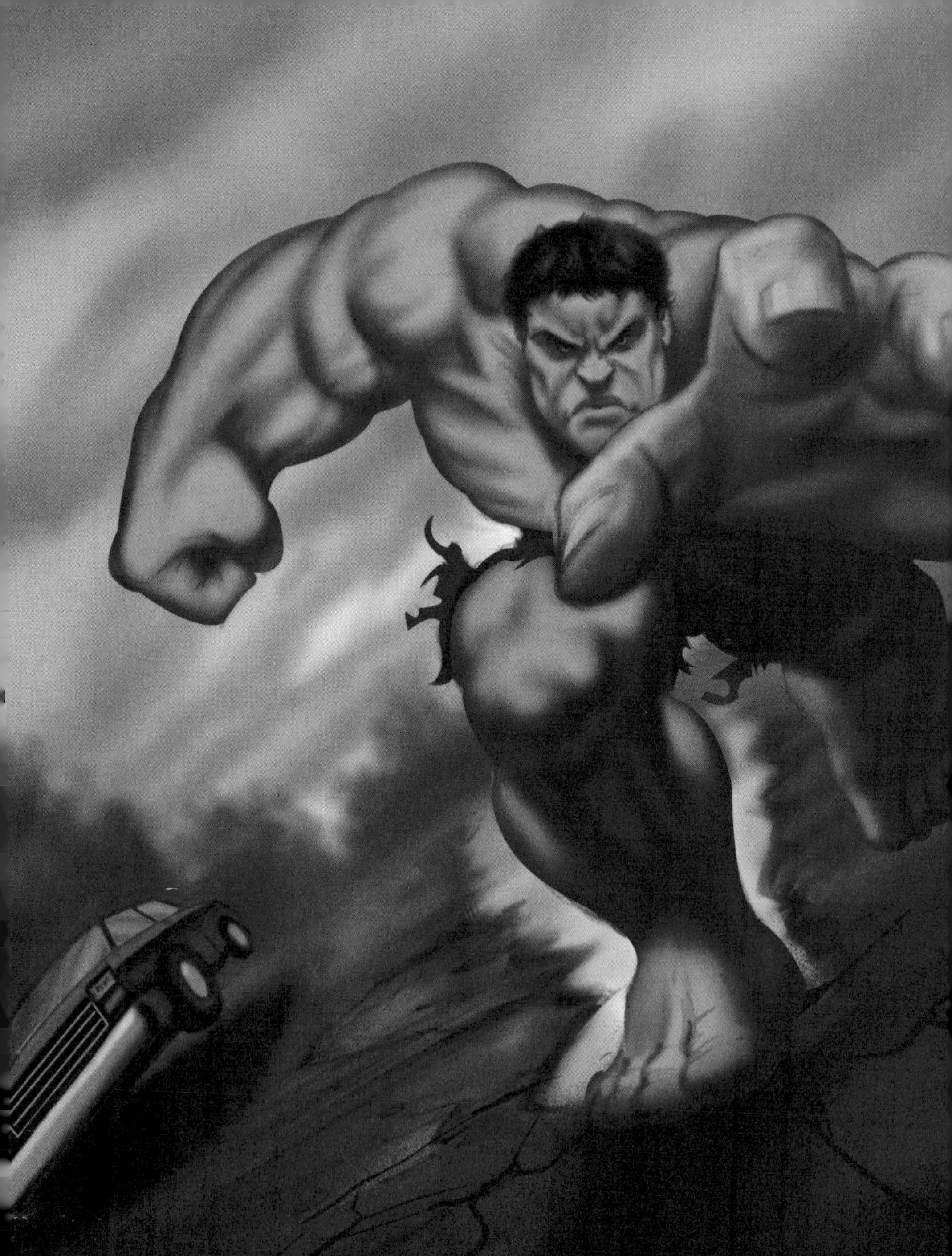

When the Hulk runs,
the ground quakes.

Buildings tumble.
Bridges shake.

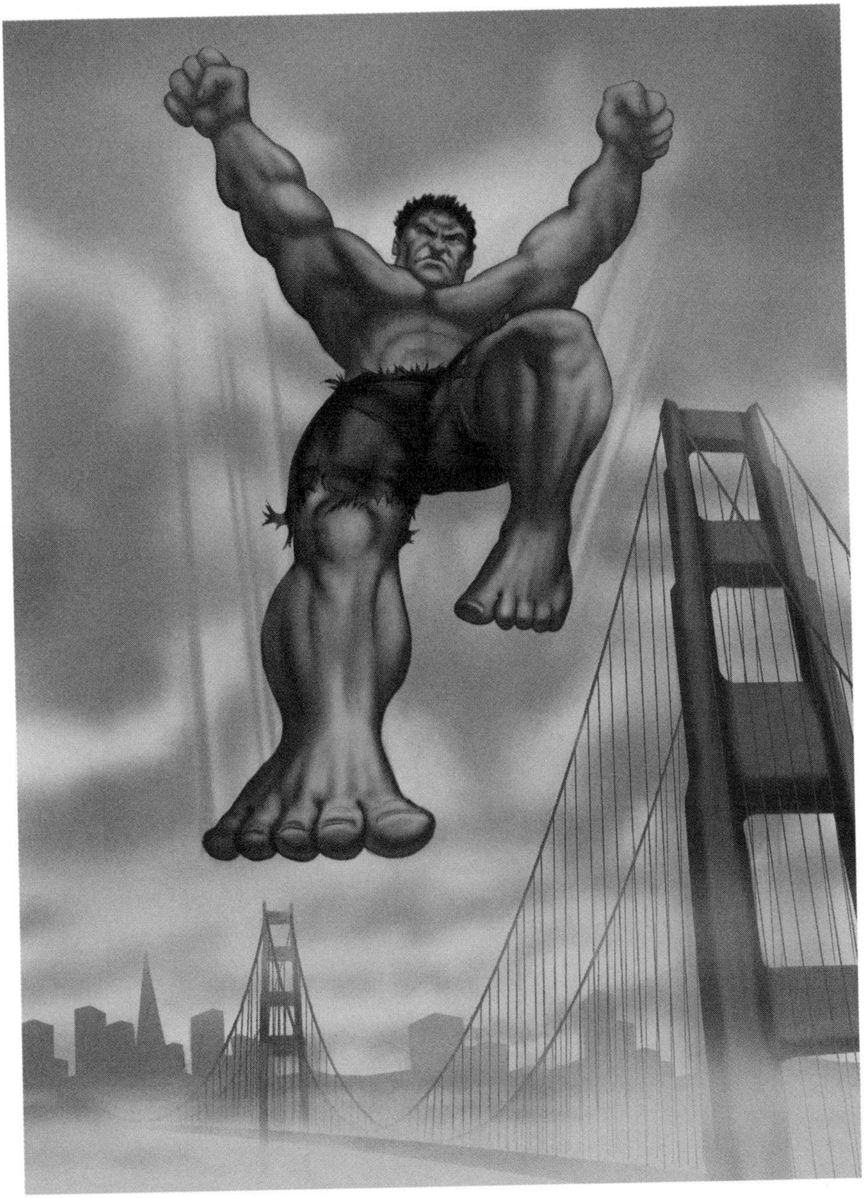

Once I begin to turn into the Hulk,
there's nothing I can do.
The Hulk is the one who is in control.

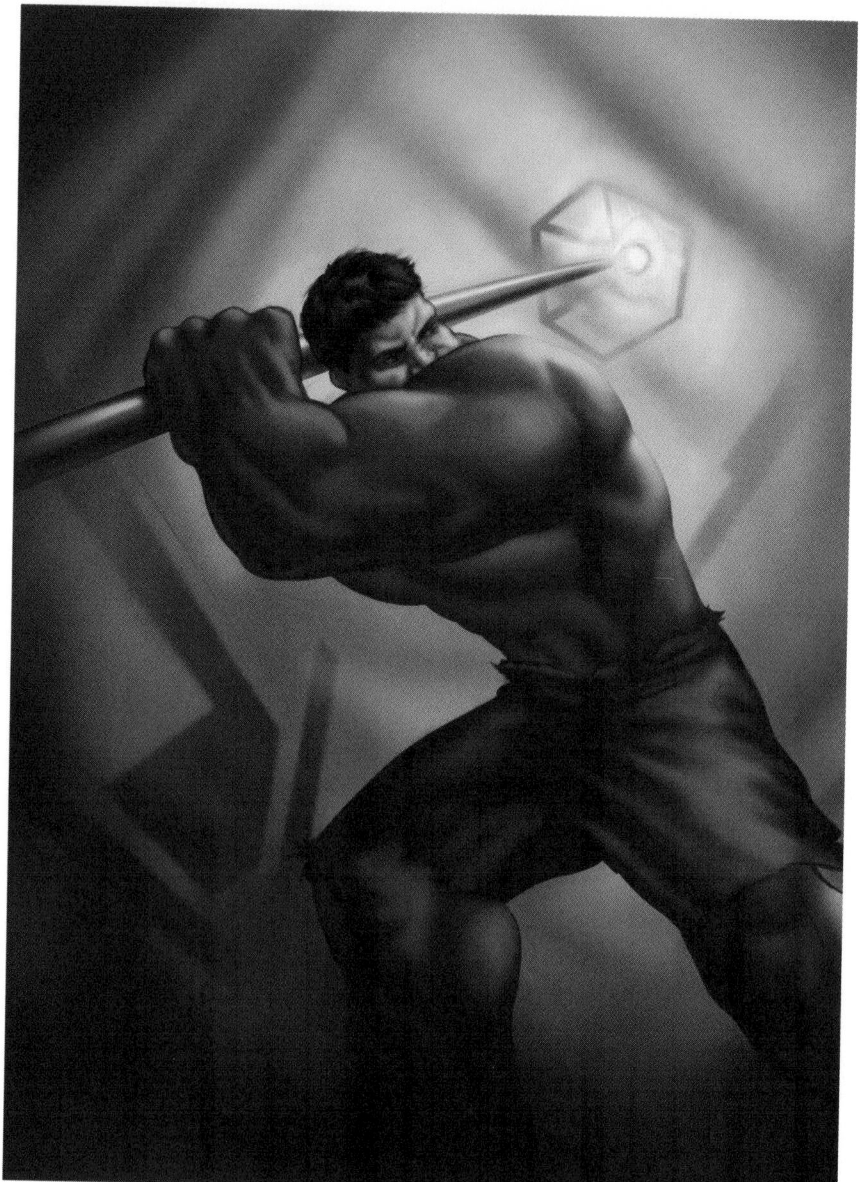

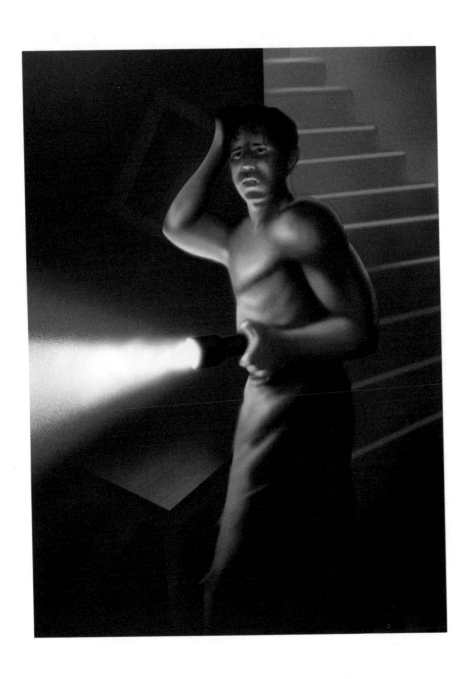

When I change back,
I can't remember being the Hulk.

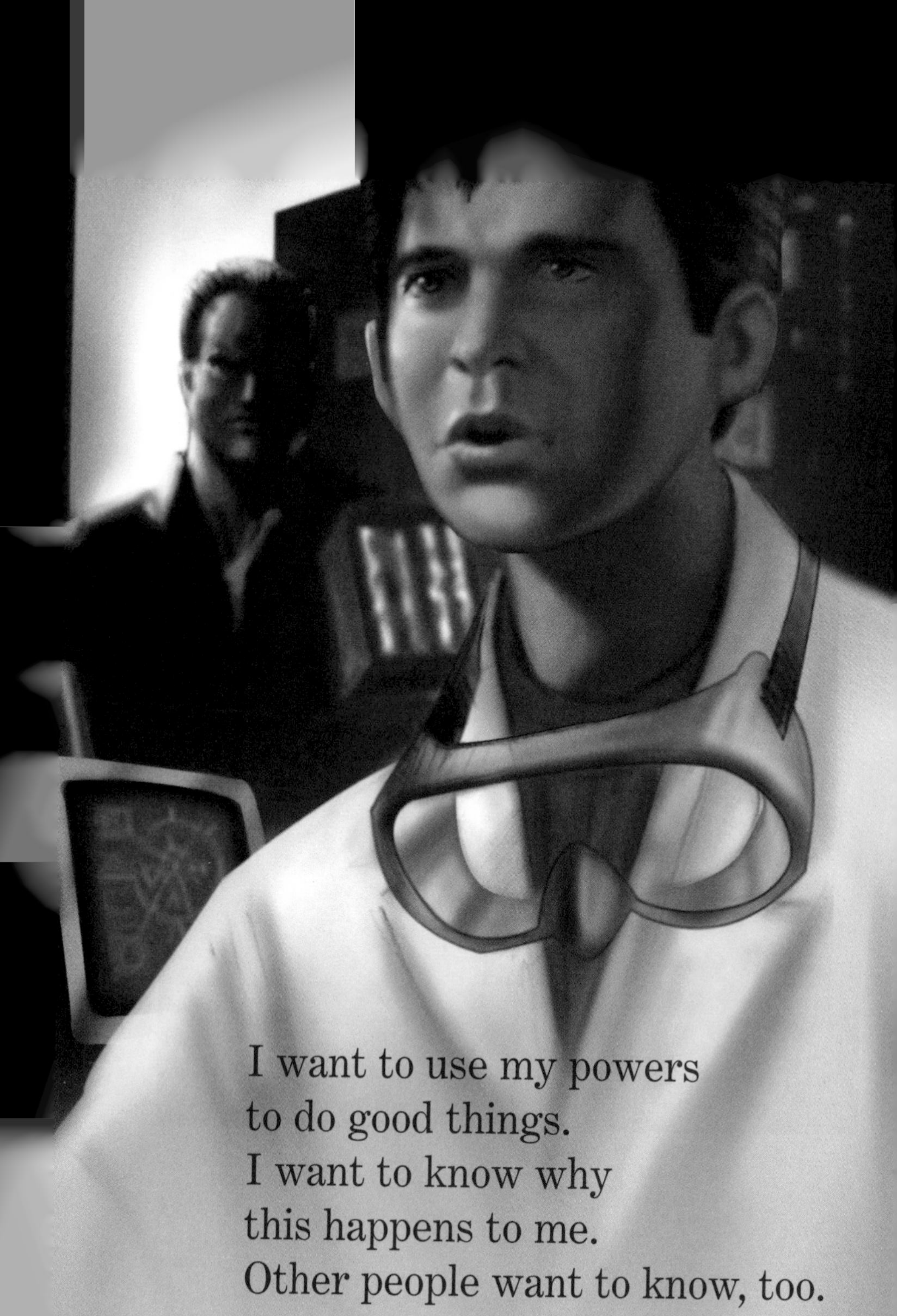

I want to use my powers
to do good things.
I want to know why
this happens to me.
Other people want to know, too.

But the others don't care
about doing good things.

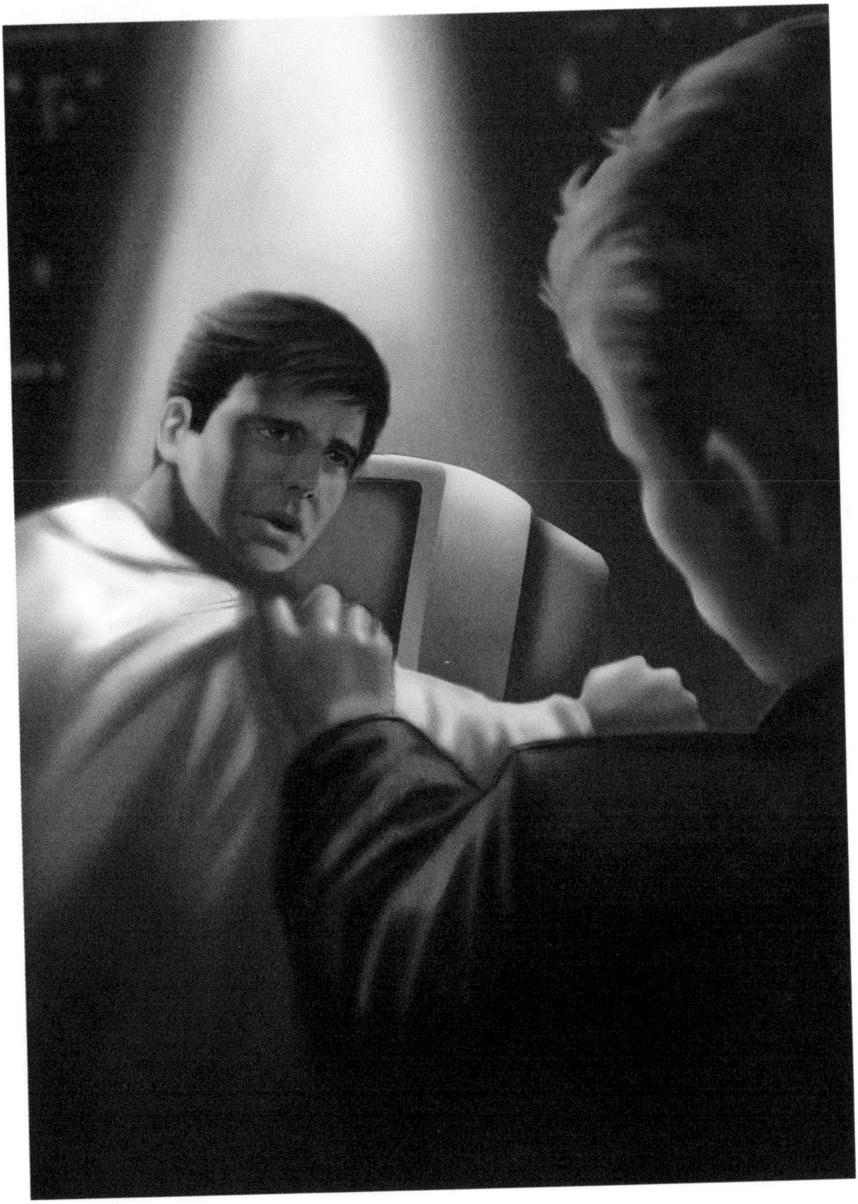

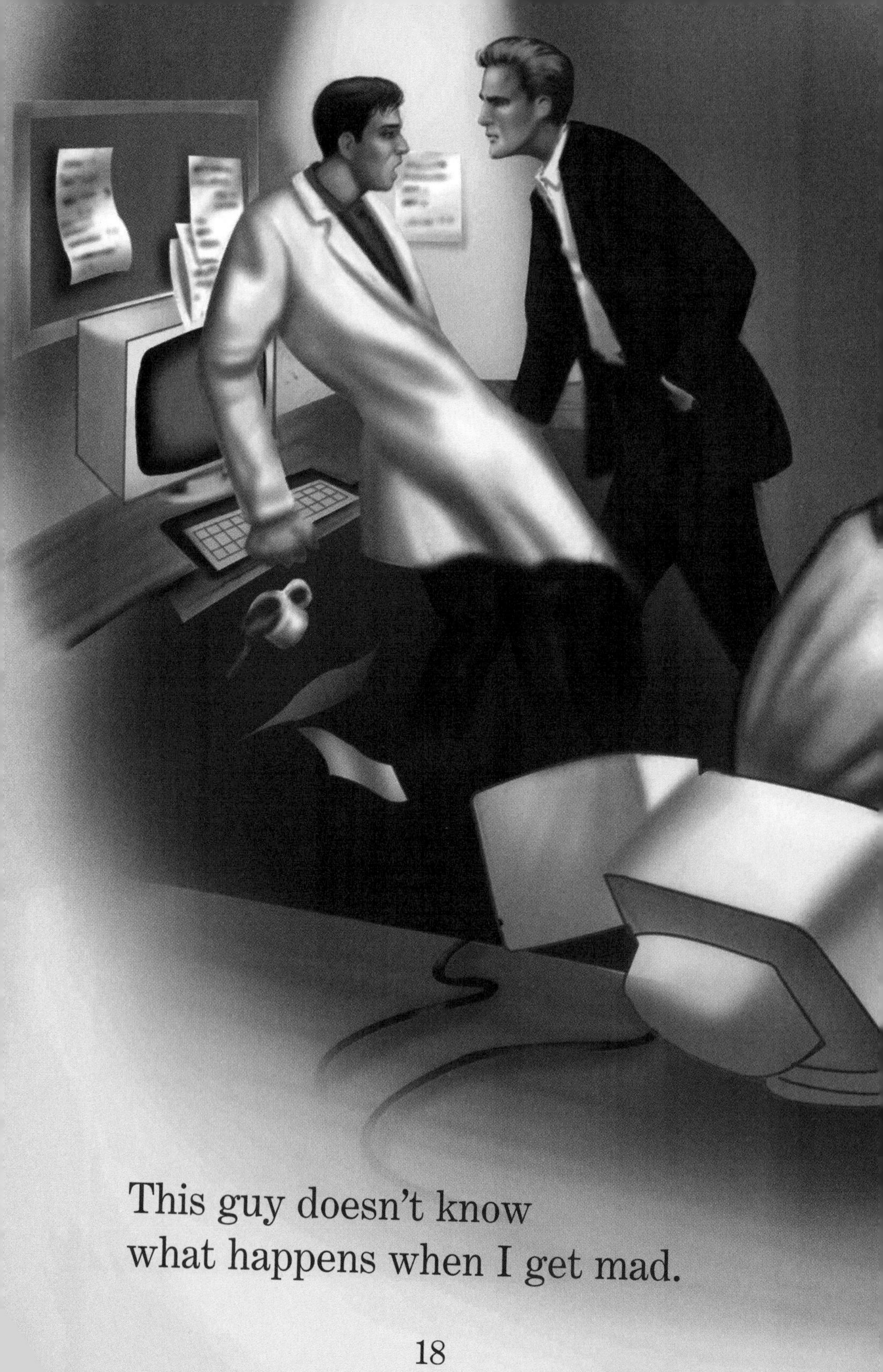

This guy doesn't know
what happens when I get mad.

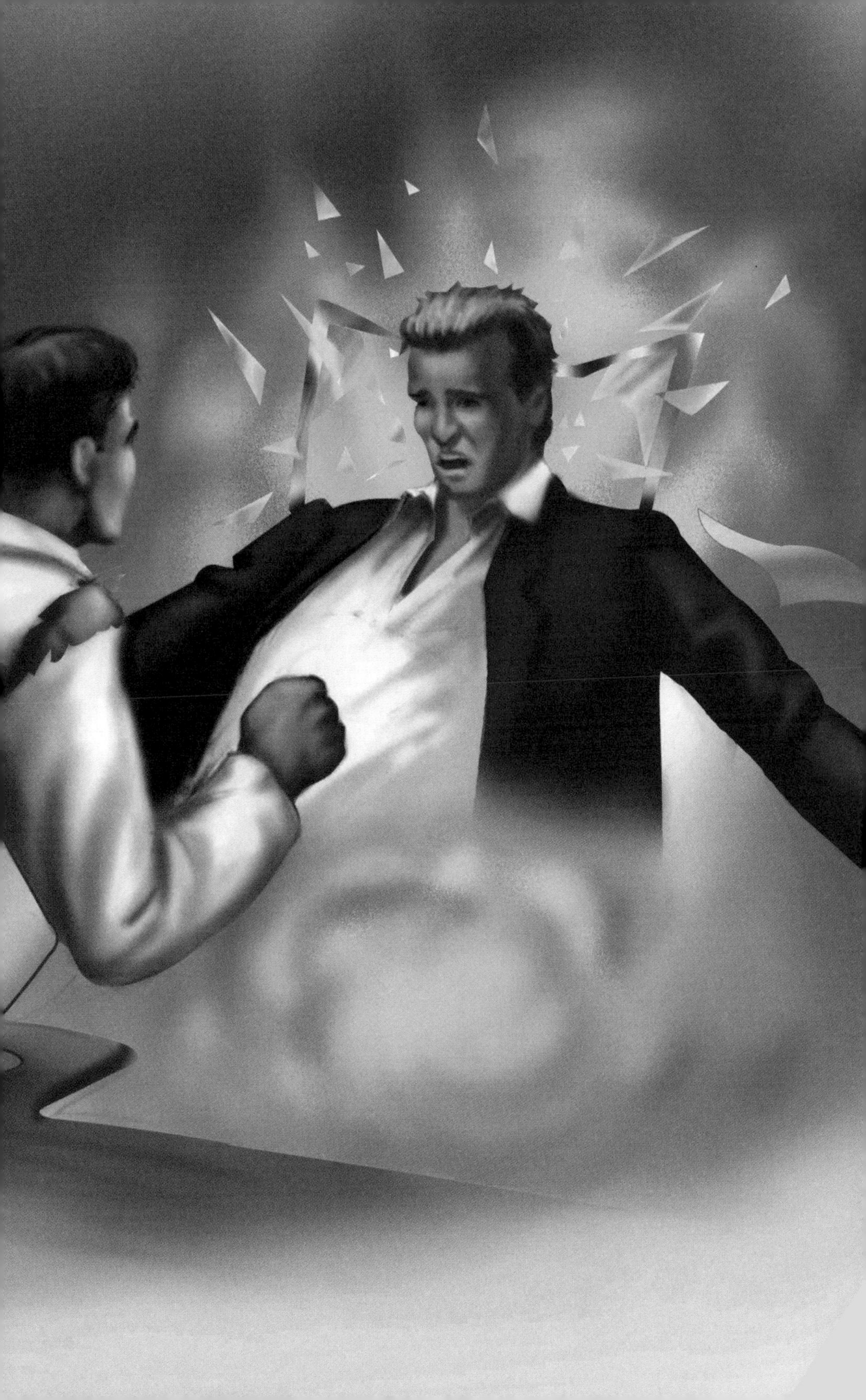

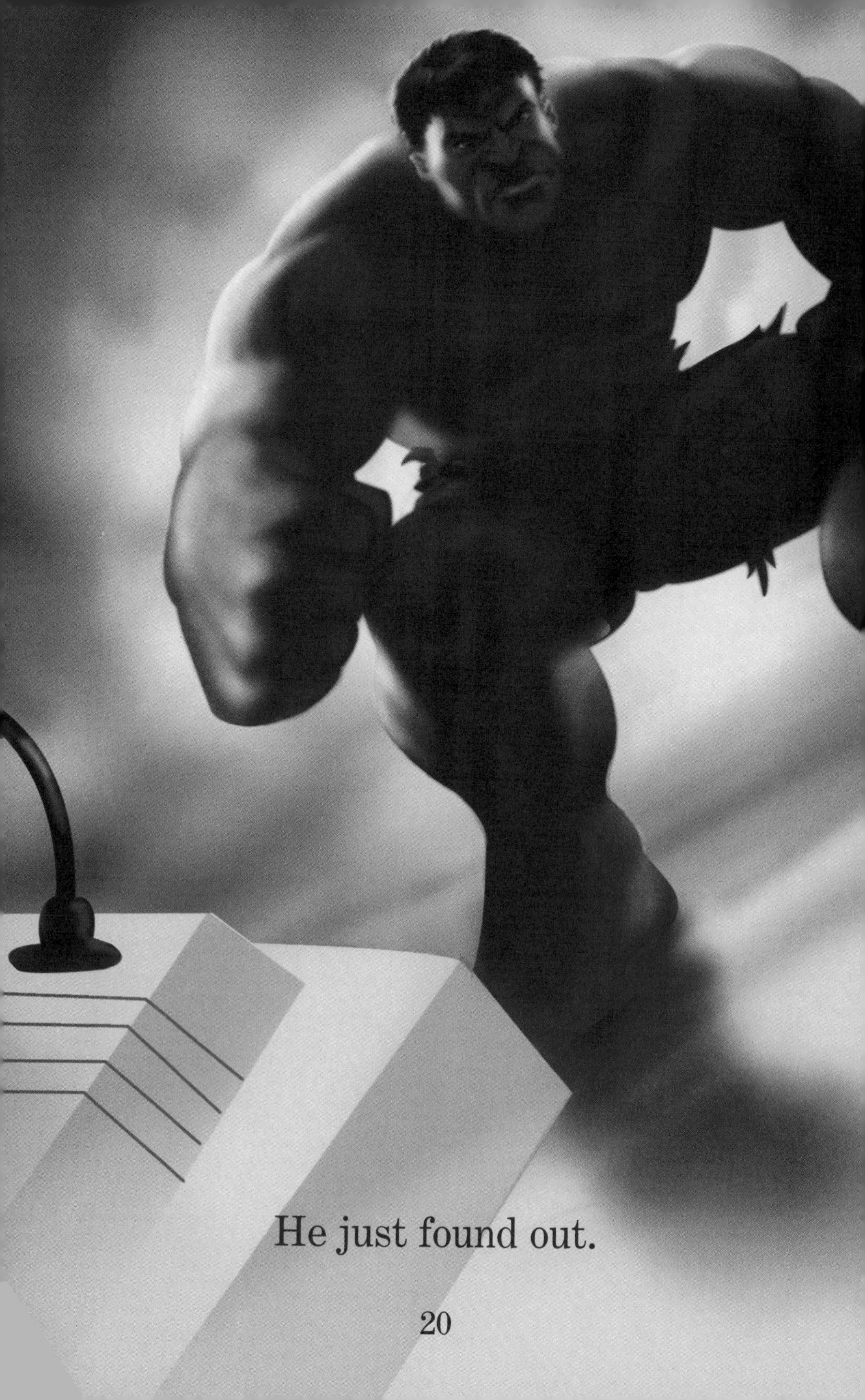

He just found out.

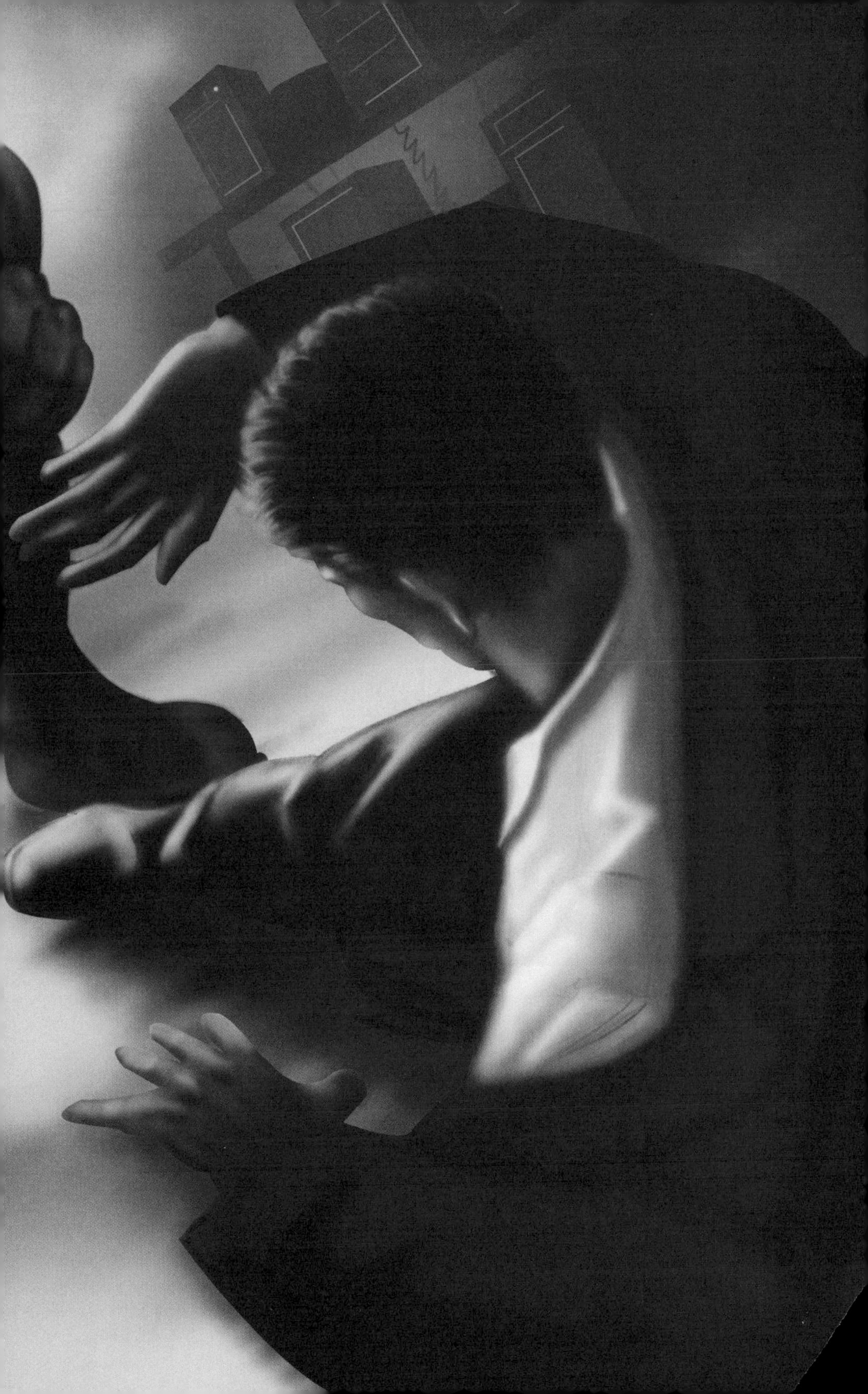

I watch out for my friends,
and so does the Hulk.
When someone hurts a friend,
I get mad.
And you know what that means.

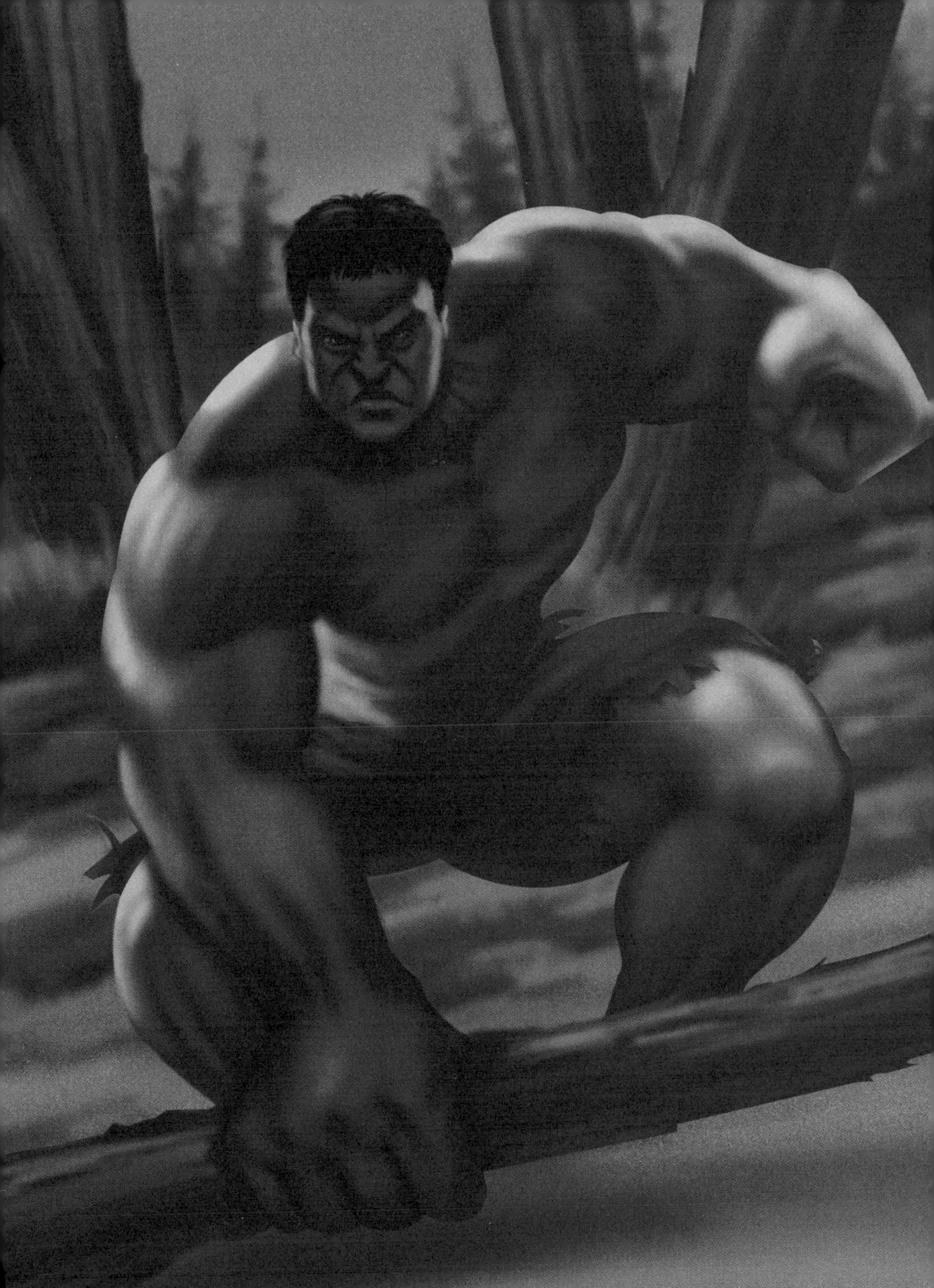

Here comes the Hulk!

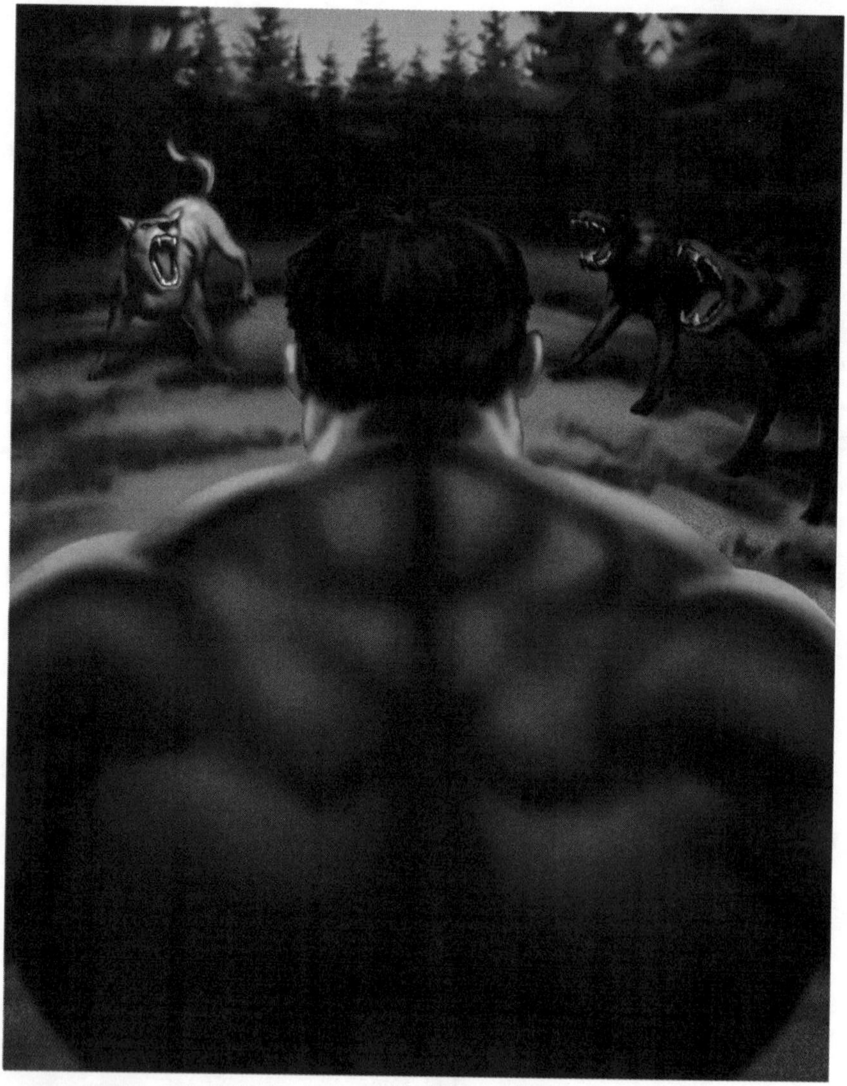

These dogs aren't exactly
man's best friends.
But three against one
is no problem for the Hulk.

This will be over
before you can say "One . . .

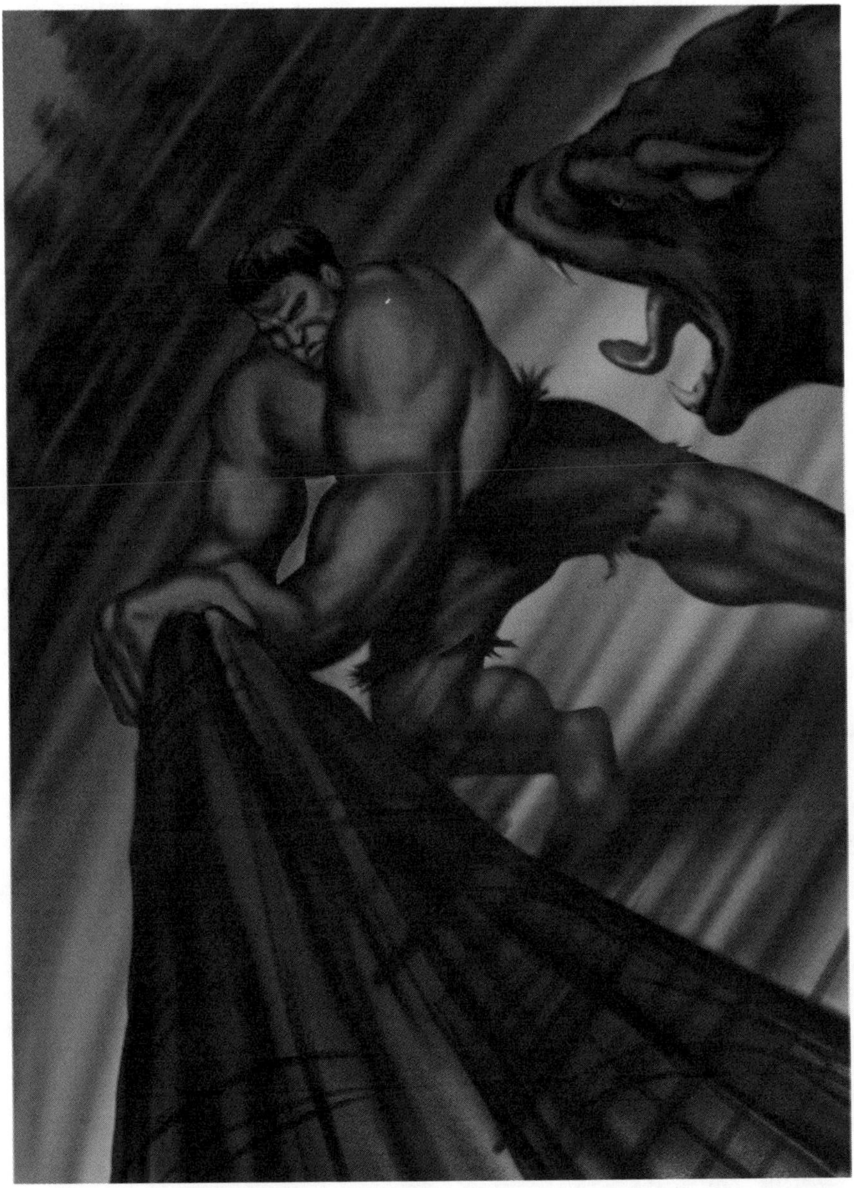

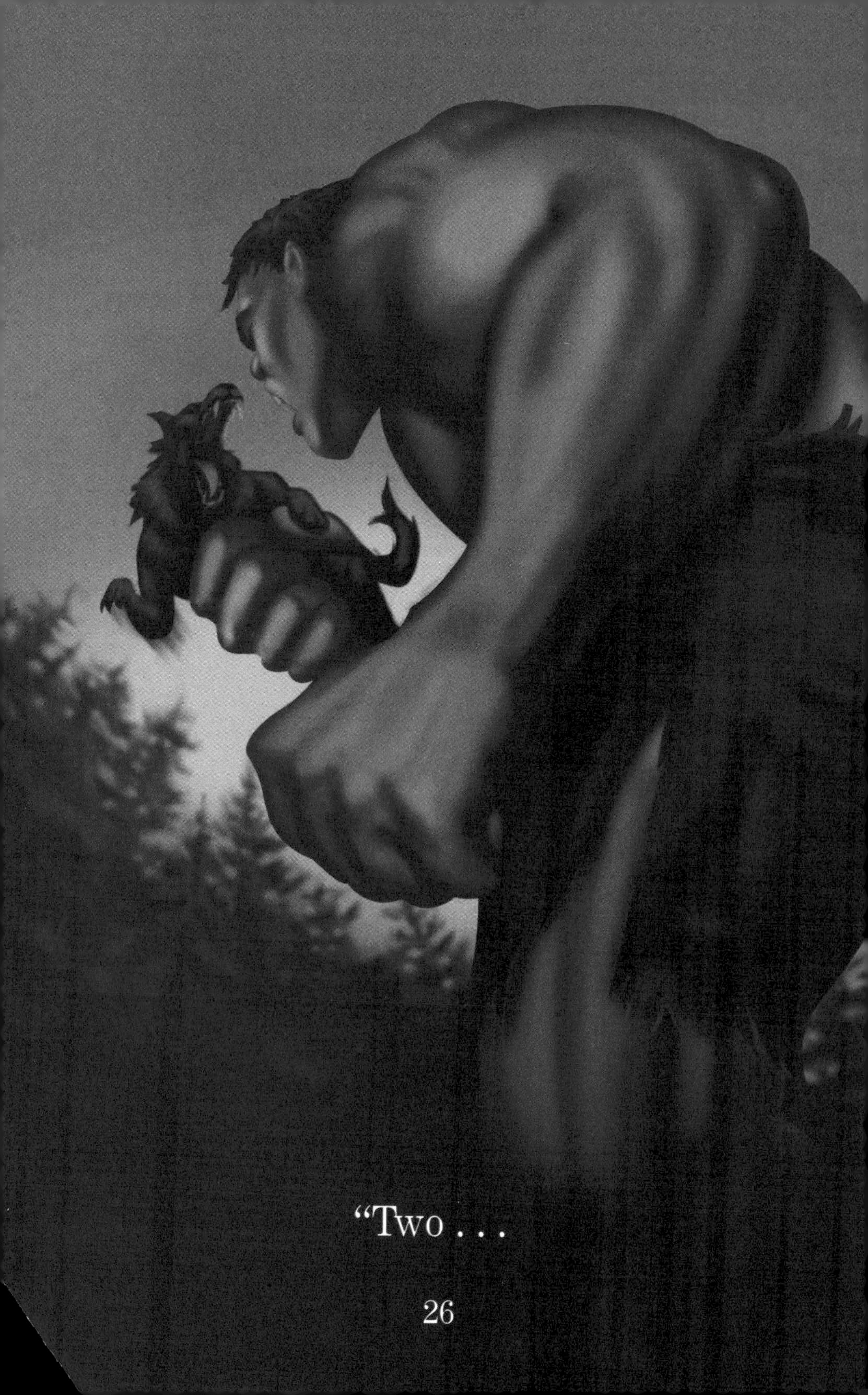

“Two . . .

“Three.”
The Hulk wins again.

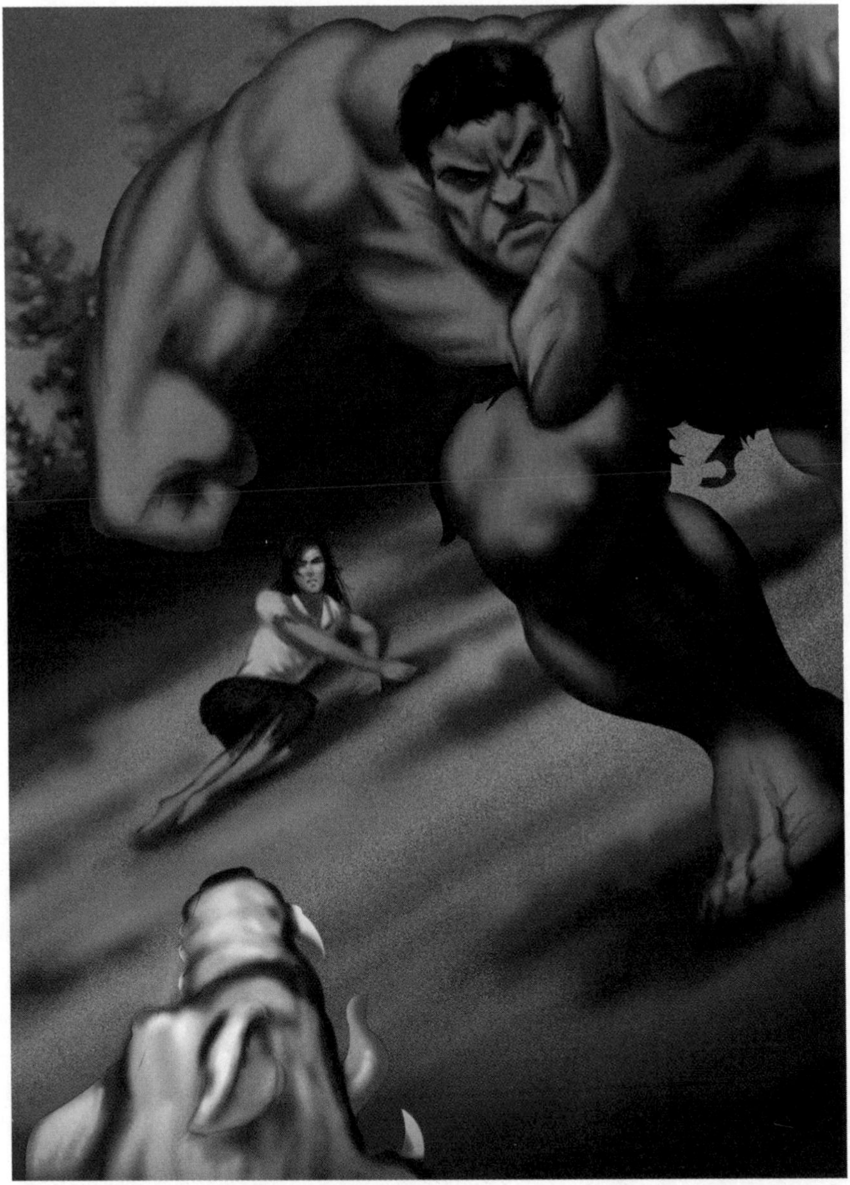

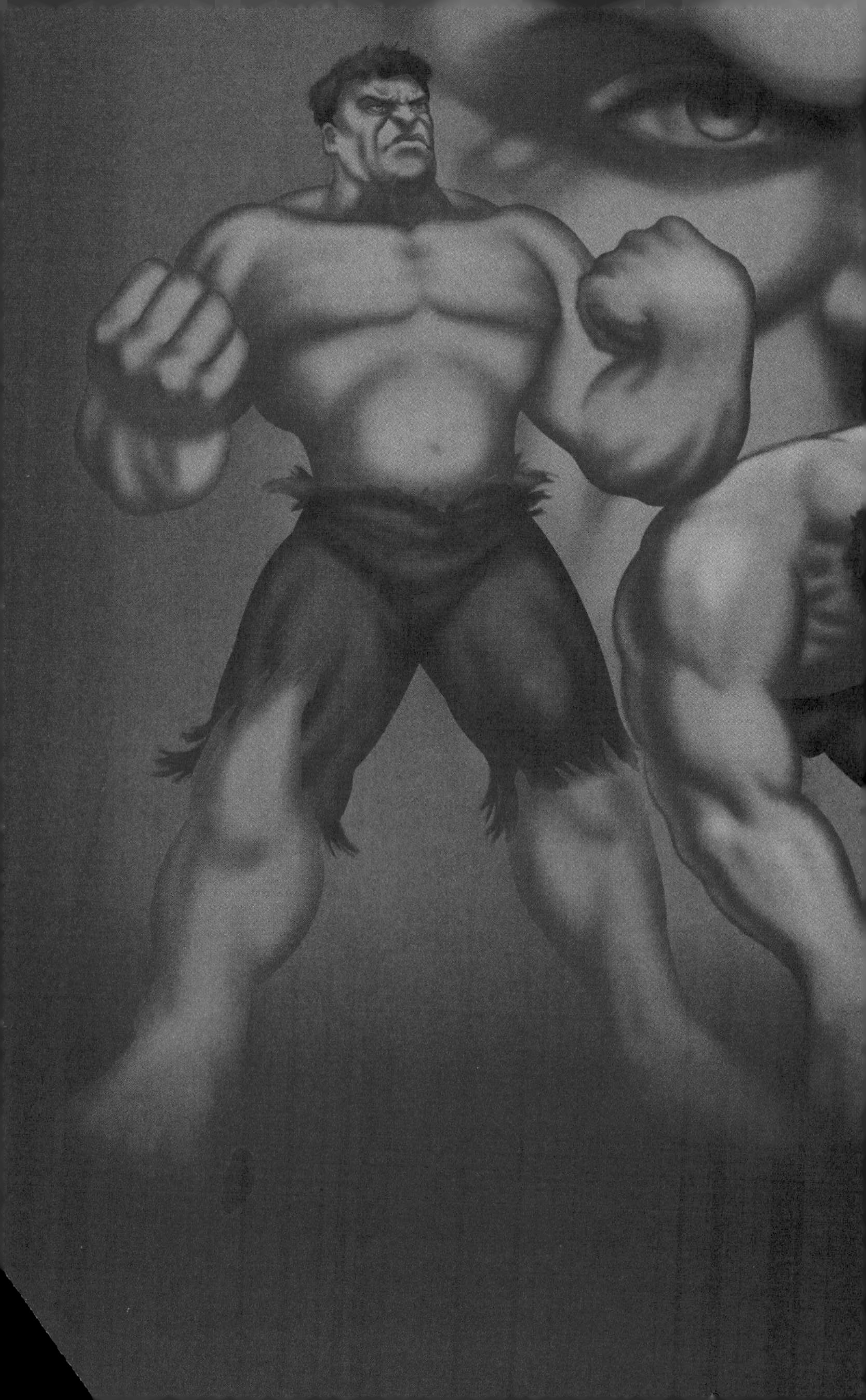

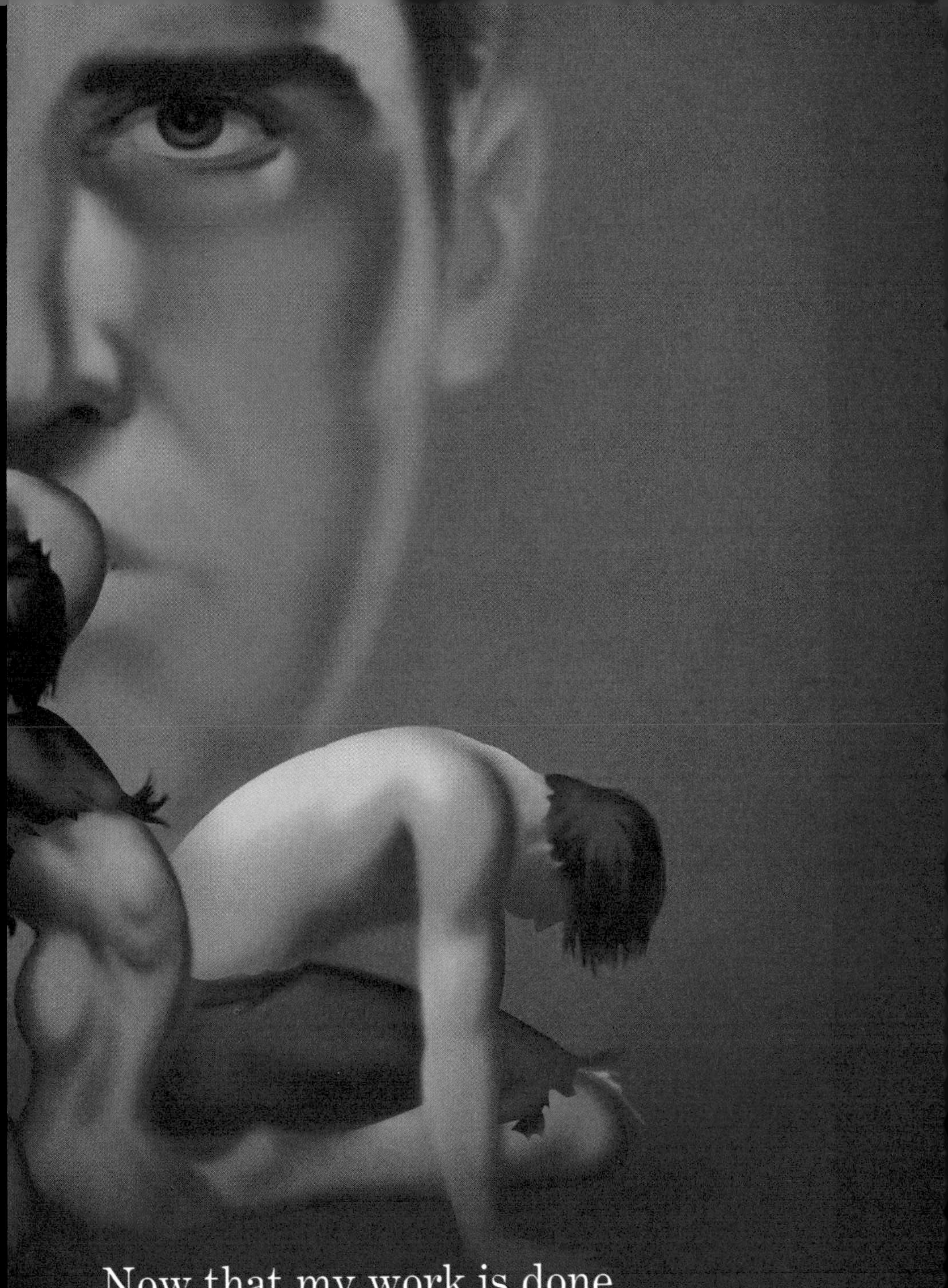

Now that my work is done,
my anger is gone, and so is the Hulk.

I am once again
living the life of a scientist—
one of the good guys.
Until someone makes me mad
and I become . . .
the Hulk!

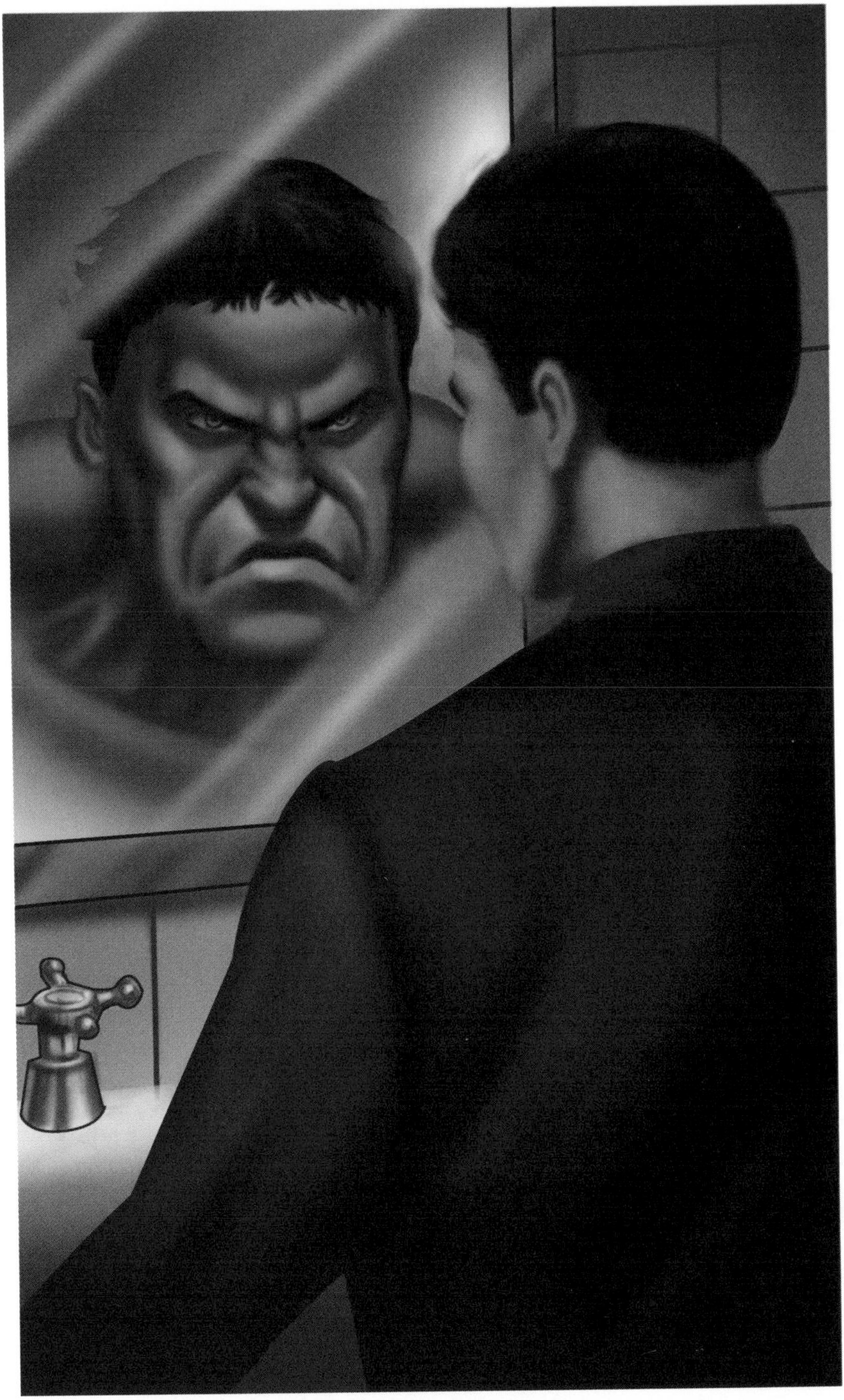

Check out this other exciting Hulk adventure!

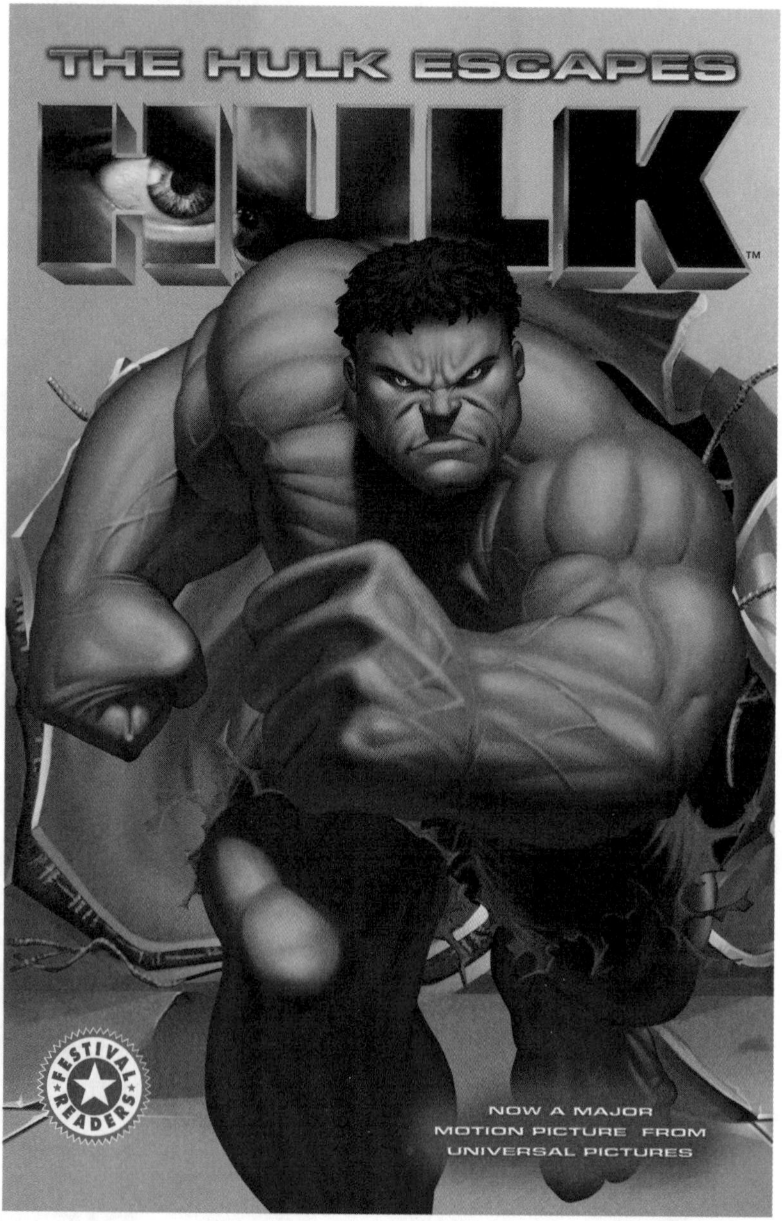
THE HULK ESCAPES
HULK™
FESTIVAL READERS
NOW A MAJOR
MOTION PICTURE FROM
UNIVERSAL PICTURES